For Mum, Dad and Val ~ SP

Flat 2b,
1091 Stilton Row,
City Heights,
Mouseville

Dear Country Mouse,
Please come and stay in the
city with me. There's so much
to do and so much to see.
You will love it!
See you soon.

Love, City Mouse X

Country Mouse was leaving his quiet little home. He was going to the Big City.

His heart raced, as the countryside swept by in a blur of leafy green.

The city took his breath away.

There were so many people . . .

. . . but no one stopped to show him the way.

Country Mouse was on his own.

And the streets all looked the same . . .

strange . . .

dark . . .

. . . and **dangerous!**

He needed a friend – fast!
And he showed up just in time.

Suddenly the city
didn't feel so strange.

"You'll love it here,"
said City Mouse.

And he did!

The city was amazing!

The city was intoxicating!

The city was magnificent!

But when Country Mouse gazed across the rooftops and saw the green hills of his home, he began to feel sad.

"I miss my countryside," he said, and he told his friend all about it – how beautiful it was, how peaceful.

He loved City Mouse
and he loved the city.

But it was time to go home.

Country Mouse lay out on the soft, green grass and smiled. "It's good to be back!" he said. "There's just no place like home."